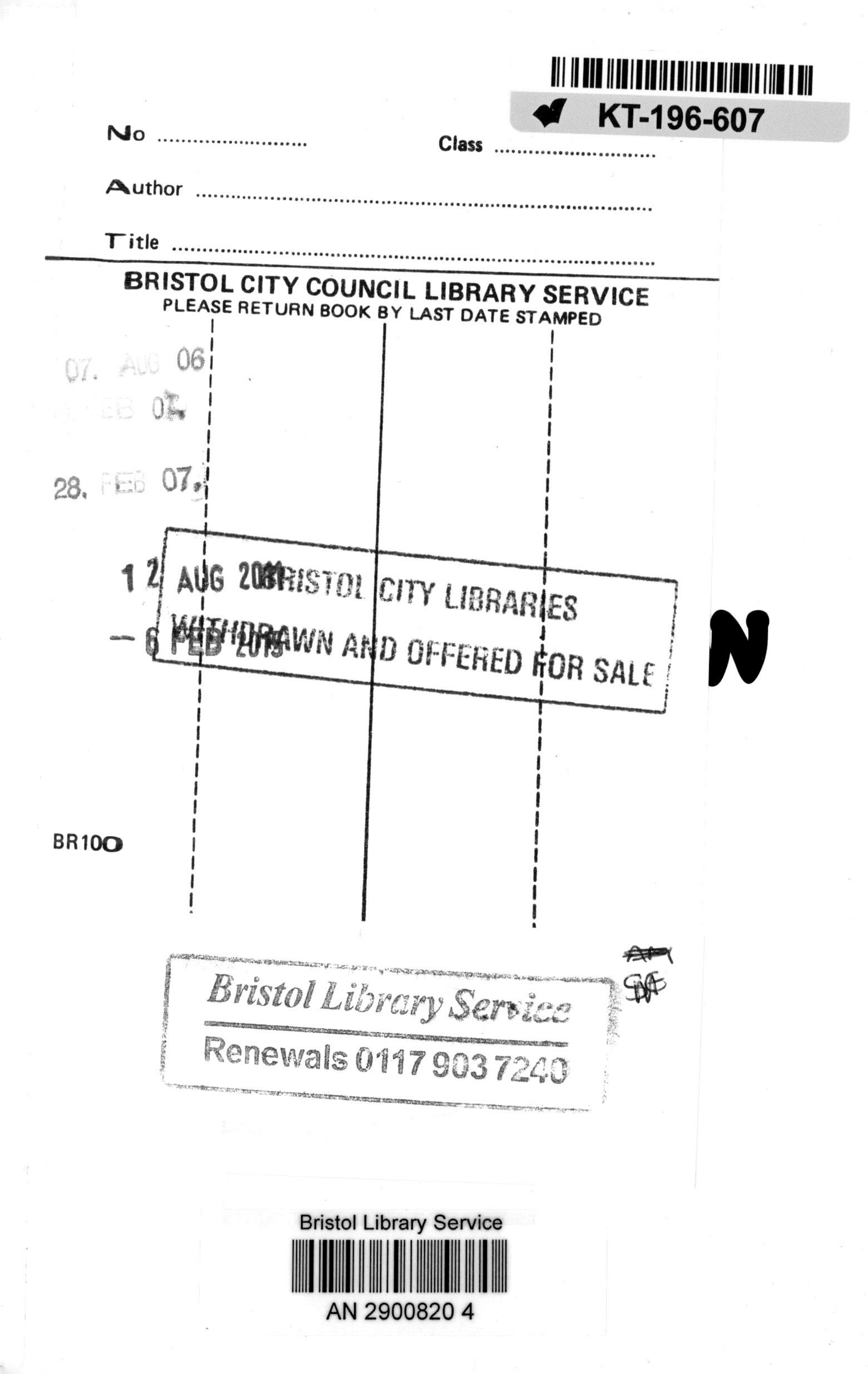

First published in 2001 by
Franklin Watts
96 Leonard Street
London
EC2A 4XD

Franklin Watts Australia
45-51 Huntley Street
Alexandria
NSW 2015

A CIP catalogue record for this book is available from the British Library.

ISBN 0 7496 3928 8 (hbk)
ISBN 0 7496 4082 0 (pbk)

Series Editor: Louise John
Series Advisor: Dr Barrie Wade
Series Designer: Jason Anscomb

Printed in Hong Kong

The Lazy Scarecrow

by Jillian Powell

Illustrated by Jayne Coughlin

FRANKLIN WATTS
LONDON•SYDNEY

A scarecrow stood in the middle of a field.

His job was to stop the birds eating the seeds.

But he was a very lazy scarecrow.

Soon, the birds came and began to eat the seeds.

"I don't care!" the scarecrow said.

They sat on his hat and on his arms.

Spring turned to summer
and the field was bare.
All the seeds had gone!

The scarecrow was sad.
It was hot and the wind
blew dust into his eyes.

He waved his arms around and around.

The farmer came past in his truck.

That scarecrow is working hard now, he thought.

So, the farmer moved the scarecrow to a better field.

Green barley
danced around the
scarecrow's feet.

A bird came and this time the scarecrow waved his arms to scare it away.

"Go away!" he shouted.
"Leave my barley alone!"

In the autumn, the barley was tall and strong.

It was the best harvest
the farmer had ever had.

He was so pleased, he gave the scarecrow a new hat for the winter.

The scarecrow was happy.
I will never be lazy again,
he thought.

Leapfrog has been specially designed to fit the requirements of the National Literacy Strategy. It offers real books for beginning readers by top authors and illustrators.

There are 25 Leapfrog stories to choose from:

The Bossy Cockerel

Written by Margaret Nash,
illustrated by Elisabeth Moseng

Bill's Baggy Trousers

Written by Susan Gates,
illustrated by Anni Axworthy

Mr Spotty's Potty

Written by Hilary Robinson,
illustrated by Peter Utton

Little Joe's Big Race

Written by Andy Blackford,
illustrated by Tim Archbold

The Little Star

Written by Deborah Nash,
illustrated by Richard Morgan

The Cheeky Monkey

Written by Anne Cassidy,
illustrated by Lisa Smith

Selfish Sophie

Written by Damian Kelleher,
illustrated by Georgie Birkett

Recycled!

Written by Jillian Powell,
illustrated by Amanda Wood

Felix on the Move

Written by Maeve Friel,
illustrated by Beccy Blake

Pippa and Poppa

Written by Anne Cassidy,
illustrated by Philip Norman

Jack's Party

Written by Ann Bryant,
illustrated by Claire Henley

The Best Snowman

Written by Margaret Nash,
illustrated by Jörg Saupe

Eight Enormous Elephants

Written by Penny Dolan,
illustrated by Leo Broadley

Mary and the Fairy

Written by Penny Dolan,
illustrated by Deborah Allwright

The Crying Princess

Written by Anne Cassidy,
illustrated by Colin Paine

Cinderella

Written by Barrie Wade,
illustrated by Julie Monks

The Three Little Pigs

Written by Maggie Moore,
illustrated by Rob Hefferan

The Three Billy Goats Gruff

Written by Barrie Wade,
illustrated by Nicola Evans

Goldilocks and the Three Bears

Written by Barrie Wade,
illustrated by Kristina Stephenson

Jack and the Beanstalk

Written by Maggie Moore,
illustrated by Steve Cox

Little Red Riding Hood

Written by Maggie Moore,
illustrated by Paula Knight

Jasper and Jess

Written by Anne Cassidy,
illustrated by François Hall

The Lazy Scarecrow

Written by Jillian Powell,
illustrated by Jayne Coughlin

The Naughty Puppy

Written by Jillian Powell,
illustrated by Summer Durantz

Freddie's Fears

Written by Hilary Robinson,
illustrated by Ross Collins